Distributed to Schools and Libraries
in the United States by
ENCYCLOPAEDIA BRITANNICA EDUCATIONAL CORP.
310 S. Michigan Avenue
Chicago, Illinois 60604

Library of Congress Cataloging-in-Publication Data
A little book of courage/illustrations by Penny Dann
Penny Dann
p. cm
Summary: Quotations about courage
taken from famous sources.
ISBN 1-56766-094-0
1. Courage -Quotations, maxims, etc - Juvenile literature.
[1. Courage -Quotations, maxims, etc.] Dann, Penny, ill.
BJ1533. C8L57 1993   93 - 6640
179'. 6 - dc20   CIP/AC

A Little Book of COURAGE

Pictures by Penny Dann

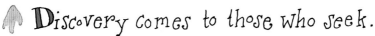

Discovery comes to those who seek.

For a very brave boy...
Tommy B.

Everyone possesses the power to enrich life. Our effectiveness, however, depends upon our ability to openly express our thoughts. This little book is intended to help us do that. The following pages contain a variety of thoughts concerning courage. Read the words carefully. Think of ways they can improve your life. Then share your thoughts about courage – and any other subject under the sun – with your friends.

You may be disappointed if you fail, but you are doomed if you don't try.

Beverly Sills

Nothing is impossible to a willing mind.

Chinese Proverb

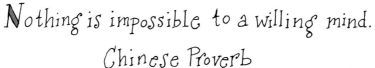

Little strokes
fell great oaks.

Benjamin Franklin

An acorn is an oak tree in the making.
Erik Butterworth

Turn stumbling blocks into stepping stones.

Anonymous

Sometimes the simplest things in life seem like the most difficult.

Ray Kroc

The more difficult the obstacle, the stronger one becomes after hurdling it.

Norman Vincent Peale

Birds shed their feathers to grow better ones.

J. Jelinek

Behold the turtle.
He only makes progress
when he sticks his neck out.

James Bryan Conant

There are times when it requires more courage to stand still than to go forward.

John Oliver

No one can make you feel inferior
without your consent.

Eleanor Roosevelt

When you must, you can.

Jewish saying

How do you eat an elephant?
One bite at a time.

Anonymous

If at first you don't succeed, try, try again.

Aesop

Always act the part and you can become
whatever you wish to become!

Max Reinhart

One can never consent to creep when one feels an impulse to soar.

Helen Keller

...and kids too!

A man can succeed at almost anything for which he has unlimited enthusiasm.

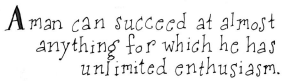

Charles Schwab

I'm not afraid of storms, for
I'm learning how to sail my ship.

Jo in "Little Women"

Man cannot discover new oceans
until he has courage to lose sight of the shore.

Ralph Waldo Emerson

If you have made mistakes...
there is always another chance for you...
you may have a fresh start any moment you choose
for this thing we call "failure" is not the
falling down, but the staying down.

Mary Pickford

Courage is not the absence of fear,
it is the mastery of it.

Ron Ball

He who never made a mistake
never made a discovery.

Samuel Smiles

Hitch your wagon to a star.

Ralph Waldo Emerson

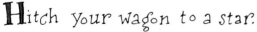

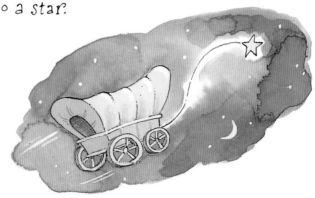

It's easy to be brave from a safe distance.
Aesop

He who does not dare,
will not get his share.

Jewish saying

It is necessary to try to surpass
one's self always; this occupation
ought to last as long as life.

Christina

When you have no choice at least be brave.

Jewish saying

You can't be brave if you've only had wonderful things happen to you.

Mary Tyler Moore

What we do need is endless courage.

Katherine Anne Porter

Theodore Engstrom